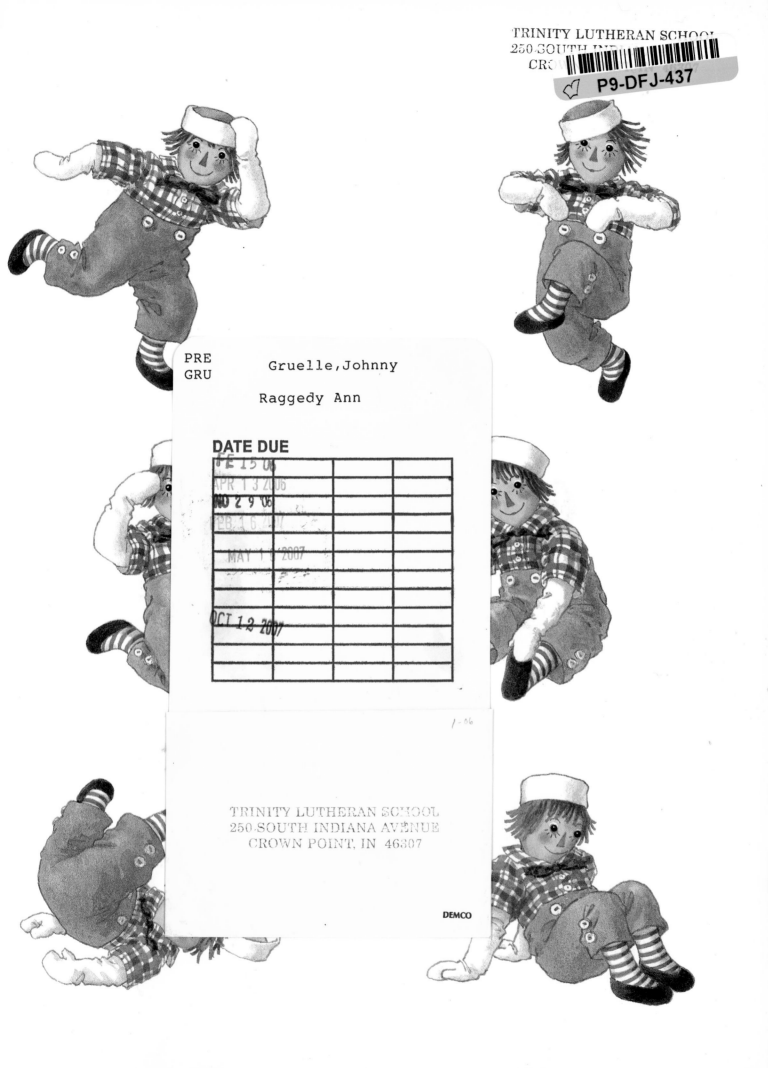

PRE
GRU

Gruelle, Johnny

Raggedy Ann

DATE DUE

FE 15 06			
APR 1 3 2006			
NO 2 9 06			
EB 1 6			
MAY 1 2007			
OCT 1 2 2007			

1-06

DEMCO

MY FIRST
Raggedy

Ann

Raggedy Ann

and Andy

and the Camel with the

Wrinkled Knees

ADAPTED FROM THE STORY BY

JOHNNY GRUELLE

ILLUSTRATED BY JAN PALMER

SIMON & SCHUSTER BOOKS FOR YOUNG READERS

SIMON & SCHUSTER BOOKS FOR YOUNG READERS
An imprint of Simon & Schuster Children's Publishing Division
1230 Avenue of the Americas, New York, New York 10020

Copyright 1924 by P. F. Volland Co.
Copyright renewed 1951 by Myrtle Gruelle
Adaptation copyright © 1998 by Simon & Schuster, Inc.
Illustrations copyright © 1998 by Simon & Schuster, Inc.

Book design by Lee Wade
The text for this book is set in Fairfield LH.
The illustrations are rendered in Winsor and Newton ink and watercolor.
Printed and bound in the United States of America
First Edition
10 9 8 7 6 5 4 3 2 1

Library of Congress Cataloging-in-Publication Data

Gruelle, Johnny, 1880-1938.
    Raggedy Ann and Andy and the camel with the wrinkled knees / adapted from the story by Johnny
Gruelle; illustrated by Jan Palmer.
    p.   cm.
    Summary: The toy camel helps Raggedy Ann and Andy find their friend, the missing doll,
Babette, and vanquish some pirates in the process.
    ISBN 0-689-81120-9
    1. Dolls—Fiction.
[E]—21
97-00002

The History of Raggedy Ann

One day, a little girl named Marcella discovered an old rag doll in her attic. Because Marcella was often ill and had to spend much of her time at home, her father, a writer named Johnny Gruelle, looked for ways to keep her entertained. He was inspired by Marcella's rag doll, which had bright shoe-button eyes and red yarn hair. The doll became known as Raggedy Ann.

Knowing how much Marcella adored Raggedy Ann, Johnny Gruelle wrote stories about the doll. He later collected the stories he had written for Marcella and published them in a series of books. He gave Raggedy Ann a brother, Raggedy Andy, and over the years the two rag dolls acquired many friends.

Raggedy Ann has been an important part of Americana for more than half a century, as well as a treasured friend to many generations of readers. After all, she is much more than a rag doll—she is a symbol of caring and love, of compassion and generosity. Her magical world is one that promises to delight children of all ages for years to come.

One day Raggedy Ann
and Andy were walking in
the deep, deep woods
when they met their friend,
the Camel with the
wrinkled knees.
The Camel's legs were so
wrinkled and soft
that he seemed almost to
fall every time he took a step.
"Wup!" Raggedy Andy said,
as he helped the Camel
sit down. "You almost fell over
that time."
"Indeed I did," said the Camel.
"My legs aren't what
they used to be."

Raggedy Ann tried to smooth out the wrinkles in the
Camel's knees, but he smiled and said,

"That won't do a bit of good. When I was brand new, I had
sticks inside each leg to keep them straight. After a few weeks
the sticks poked through my legs, so the mother of the little boy
who played with me pulled them out. Now my knees are saggy
and soft, but I'm much more comfortable when I lie down."

Raggedy Ann felt her candy heart go *thump, thump,* for she was glad to hear the Camel's story. "Maybe you can help us," she said. "Last night we heard footsteps in the nursery. Now our friend Babette, the French doll, is gone. We don't know where she is."

The Camel scratched his head with his floppiest leg. "Maybe I can help you," he said.

"I think I can find Babette," said the Camel, "if I cover my eyes with a hanky, and if I run backward to the place where I came from. You had better climb up and ride."

So Raggedy Ann and Andy climbed onto his soft flannel back. The Camel started walking slowly, then faster, until his wobbly, wrinkled legs were hitting the ground *clumpity, clumpity, clumpity* and he was running surprisingly fast.

After they had run along for ten minutes, they heard a *clip, clop,* and Raggedy Andy turned to see a funny old horse running toward them. The Camel stopped suddenly, and the horse ran straight into him. Raggedy Ann and Andy fell over the Camel's nose. The poor Camel's head was pushed flat into the ground, and his wrinkled neck was wrinkled up against his body.

The horse sat down on his back legs and sighed. "I'm so tired," he said. "I am old, and the least exercise wears me out."

Raggedy Ann and Andy were busy pulling the Camel's head back into shape and removing the hanky from his eyes so he could see. "We were running to find our friend Babette," said Raggedy Ann. "We think she was kidnapped."

"I am running away from pirates," said the tired old horse. "Maybe they have your friend." He pointed to a large tent not far away.

Very, very quietly, the dolls, the horse, and the Camel crept up to the tent. They peeked into a small hole. Inside were twelve large pirates with mustaches. And in the corner, all alone, stood Babette.

"Listen," Raggedy Ann whispered.

"Ha!" said one pirate. "I am the bravest pirate around here."

"We are all the bravest," said all of the other pirates.

"They'll all be fighting in a few minutes," said Raggedy Andy.

Then Raggedy Andy picked up a small stone, no bigger than a pea. He threw it softly into the tent, so it bounced off one pirate's shoe.

"Ow!" the pirate howled. "Who hit me?"

Raggedy Andy threw another tiny pebble, and suddenly the pirates decided that it would be safer outside the tent. There was a jam at the doorway, and the pirates all fell in a tangle of arms, legs, and heads, pulling the tent down with them.

Raggedy Ann quickly reached under the fallen tent and found Babette. She was unhurt and very happy to see her friends.

The tired old horse turned to the pirates, who had just stopped fighting. "Now you must promise to reform and not be pirates and kidnappers anymore. And then I'll give you each a lollipop." He knew that the pirates had nothing to eat all day but bread and butter and pickles. He held twelve lollipops high, so the pirates could not reach them.

"I'll stop being a pirate and be a plumber,"
cried one pirate.

"I'll stop and go into the garage business,"
another pirate shouted.

When all the pirates had said "Cross my heart!" the tired
old horse gave them each a lollipop. Then the three dolls,
the Camel, the horse, and the pirates all climbed into the
pirates' flying boat, and it jumped into the sky and sped away.

Soon the boat came to rest in the dolls' backyard. Raggedy
Ann, Raggedy Andy, and Babette said good-bye to their friends
and crept into their playroom, where all the other dolls were
sound asleep. They climbed into their beds, bounced up and
down once, and smiled. Then they fell asleep, too.